Story People

Selected Stories & Drawings of Brian Andreas

with love,

ISBN 0-9642660-4-0

The people in this book, if at one time real, are now entirely fictitious, having been subjected to a combination of a selective memory and a fertile imagination. Any resemblance to real people you might know, even if they are the author's relatives, is entirely coincidental, and is a reminder that you are imagining the incidents in this book as much as the author is.

StoryPeople
P.O. Box 7
Decorah, IA 52101
USA
800.476.7178
319.382.8060
319.382.0263 FAX

orders@storypeople.com
http://www.storypeople.com/

First edition: October, 1997

Printed at the West Coast Print Center, Berkeley, California

To my parents & grandparents, who gave me from an early age a world filled with wonder & possibility & love.

To my sons, David Quinn & Matthew Shea, for reminding me to be fearless & fierce for those who will inherit the future, & most of all, to my dearest Ellen, for reminding me to sing with all my heart.

Other books by Brian Andreas available from StoryPeople Press:

Mostly True
Still Mostly True
Going Somewhere Soon
Strange Dreams

Cover Art: Brian Andreas
Back photo: Jon Duder
Inside back photo: Chip Petersen

Introduction

The stories in this book began as hand-stamped stories on StoryPeople. I imagine that's a pretty strange way to start out a book named *StoryPeople.* What is the book about? It's about StoryPeople. What are StoryPeople? Good question.

It's been four years since I made the first StoryPerson sculpture in my studio in Berkeley & I'm still no closer to being able to describe what they are than I was on that very first day. There's a picture of one inside the back cover. Take a look at it. The first thing you'll notice is that a StoryPerson doesn't look **like** anything else. You can't say, "Oh, it looks like (whatever)". Because they don't. The fun thing I've seen happen in the past four years is that now I hear people saying that something looks like StoryPeople. But that still doesn't help those of you who are seeing this book for the very first time.

Let's see if we can go at it a different way. The stories & drawings you're about to read on these pages are selected from the first three StoryPeople books: *Mostly True* (1993), *Still Mostly True* (1994) & *Going Somewhere Soon* (1995). I did these books at the request of many of my collectors, who told me they didn't have room to own all the sculptures & prints. Even when I was willing to work out reasonable terms, they said they'd rather have a book to carry around with them.

It's hard to argue with the logic here. So, I did the books.

StoryPeople are not about the sculpture you see in the picture, though. That's what makes them difficult to describe. They're about the memories you have of your life. It's like this: have you ever looked through an old photo album? Imagine finding a picture you haven't seen for a long time & you look at it & suddenly you're remembering, no, you're seeing things that no camera on earth could capture. Like the way the clouds came in fast that day with a strange purple light & your uncle kept saying "Looks like tornado weather to me" & your aunt kept telling him he could be part of the problem, or part of the solution, it was his choice & you still haven't figured out what she meant. Like the way your sister kept tugging her jeans down when she thought no one was looking because your mother told her she wasn't going to wash them, she had enough to do, thank you very much, & that if she wanted them, she could wash them herself, so your sister did & they shrunk. Like the way your cousin tried to see how many bees he could catch in an applesauce jar & he dropped it & it broke & two yellowjackets stung him & your uncle had to take him to emergency. Like the way your grandmother kept grabbing you by the arm & whispering to you that the future was in teaching.

A picture is only a marker. It will never be the whole picture. That's not why we save pictures anyway. We keep them as a way of keeping ourselves, as a way of holding our stories safe. To look at a picture we have forgotten is to remember & treasure that memory as a part of our lives. With such a simple act, we return our stories to ourselves.

In the introduction to the first book, Mostly True, I wrote:

> *Well, here it is. Mostly true. Buy it. Read it. Send it to friends. Use it to start a conversation. Teach it to people from other countries & have them translate it. Sing your favorites to yourself in the shower. Ask your children to explain them to you. Explain it to them when you're in the car & they can't get away. When you meet someone new, have them read it to help you decide whether you want to spend any more time with them.*

When that book came out, there was only a handful of people who knew about StoryPeople. I knew that the stories in the books were powerful: they make you laugh & cry & wonder & remember. What I didn't know is that these stories would start up a chain of other stories. People reading them to each other & asking what they meant. People talking with each other about important things, like angels & children & dreams. People smiling secretly at the people around them & falling in love again. People remembering what they didn't know they forgot...

So, here it is. A selection of my favorites from the first three books put into one (though I still offer reasonable terms). Still mostly true, just like before. I hope they start you on a great adventure, the way they have me & so many others I know. Let me know how it goes...

With love,

Brian Andreas
16 October 1997

Story People

Most of the stuff
I say is true because
I saw it in a dream
& I don't have the
presence of mind
to make up lies
when I'm asleep.

Remembering

When I was 5, he said,
my family forgot & left
me at the fair. I wandered
around in the bright
sounds & smells of hot
sawdust & cotton candy
for hours. It was already
too late by the time my
parents found me.

I haven't been fit for
decent society since.

My uncle told me once
there were 3 rules for a
great opera. Make it loud,
wear flashy clothes & if
it's not going your way,
kill yourself.
It has no basis in reality,
he added. That's why I
like it.

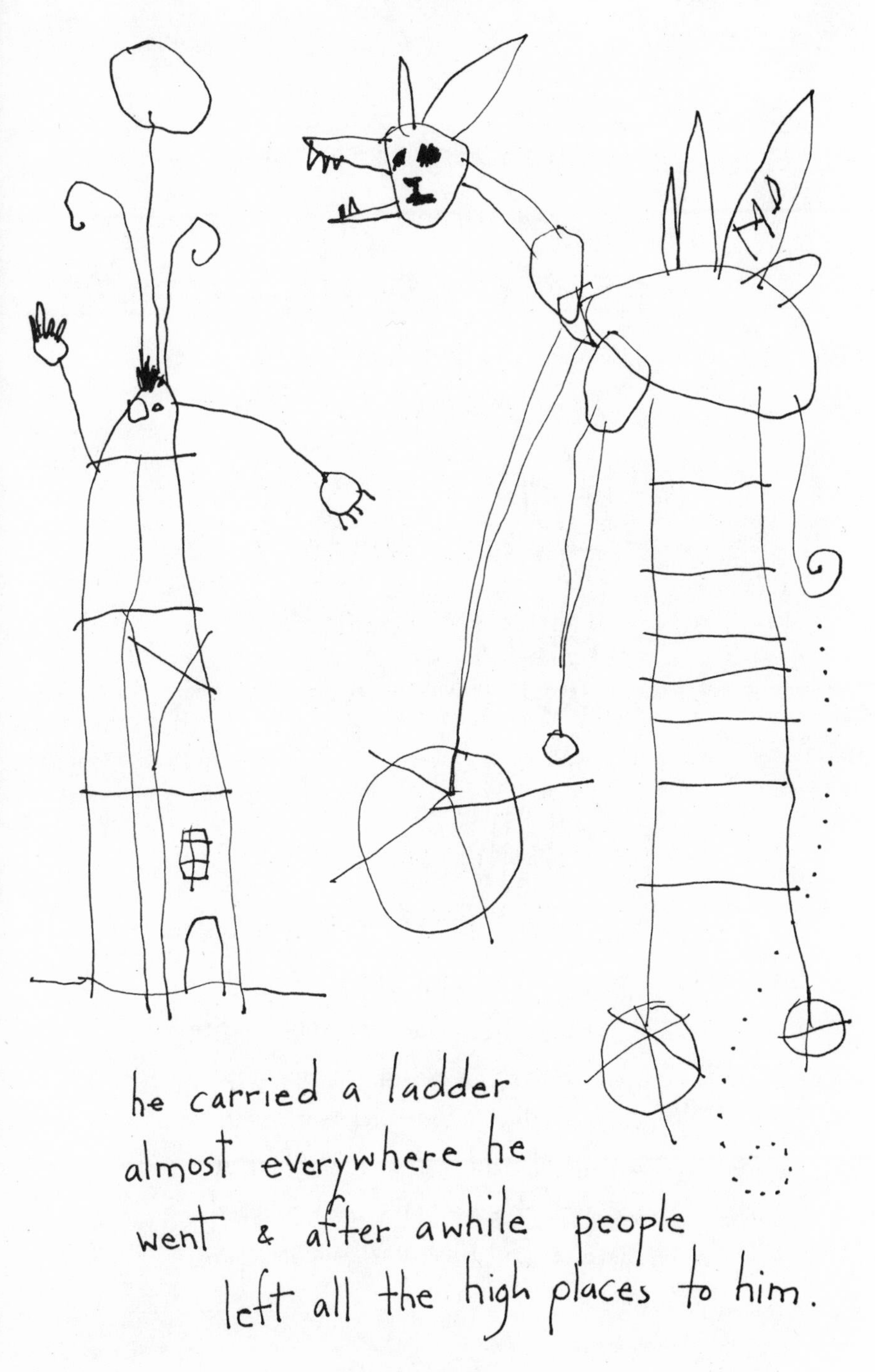
he carried a ladder
almost everywhere he
went & after awhile people
left all the high places to him.

High Places

I remember once I went to my great-grandmother's house. It was a big white house & it always smelled like slightly burned

toast & raspberry jam. She had a picture of Jesus on the wall in her living room. She told me his eyes would follow you around when you walked. I told a friend about it a while ago. He nodded & said he used to have a Chihuahua that did the same thing.

Chihuahua

He wrote secret notes to
people he hadn't met yet.
Some of them aren't even
born, he said, but we live
in a strange neighborhood
& they will need help
figuring things out & I
won't always be around
to explain it to them.

I used to eat
popcorn for
every meal,
she told me
once. It made
me feel like
I was in
the
movies
& my
life
would turn
out happy
in the end.
Did it work?
I said.
I don't know, she said,
but I like to think the
roughage counts for something.

Roughage

I will
always remember
the day when the sun
shone dark on your hair
& I forgot where we
were & kissed you
lightly on the
nose

& suddenly
there was no more secret.

I like Geography best,
he said, because your
mountains & rivers
know the secret.

Pay no attention to
boundaries.

When we lived in the city we used to leave the lights on to keep away the burglars.
Now we leave the lights off to keep away the neighbors.
My mom says it's because there's always a chance we'll like the burglars.

Neighbors

This is poison soup
to kill the bad witches,
she said.

How can you tell the
difference? I asked.

O, good witches are
very polite & say no
thank you. Bad witches
just die.

Believing My Father

My great-aunt Clara told us once about the time she was one of the Wise men in the church play & when it came to

her part she said we're here bearing frankincense, gold & myrrh, heavy on the frankincense because of that camel smell & after that her father always called it the story of the Two Wise Men & that other guy & we laughed so hard we had to pee.

There are only 2
things I take
seriously, my aunt
said once. Laughter
& my digestion.
I'm too old to
bother with more
than that.

Laughter & Digestion

I had a dream & I heard music & there were children standing around, but no one was dancing. I asked a little girl, Why not? & she said they didn't know how,

or maybe they used to but they forgot

& so I started to hop up & down & the children asked me, Is that dancing? & I laughed & said, no. that's hopping, but at least it's a start

& soon everyone was hopping & laughing & it didn't matter any more that no one was dancing:

Hopping

When I die, she said, I'm coming back as a tree with deep roots & I'll wave my leaves at the children every morning on their way to school & whisper tree songs at night in their dreams.

Trees with deep roots know about the things children need.

She waved at all the people
on the train & later, when
she saw they didn't wave back,
she started singing songs to
herself & it went that way
the whole day & she couldn't
remember having a better
time in her life.

her umbrella was
filled with rain she
had collected in her
travels & on hot summer
days she would
open it up for the
neighborhood kids & we
would splash in the
puddles
& then

ROAR!
ROAR!

it would smell like Nairobi or Tasmania
& later on we would sit on the porch &
eat ice cream & watch for tigers in
the bushes.

Tiger Rain

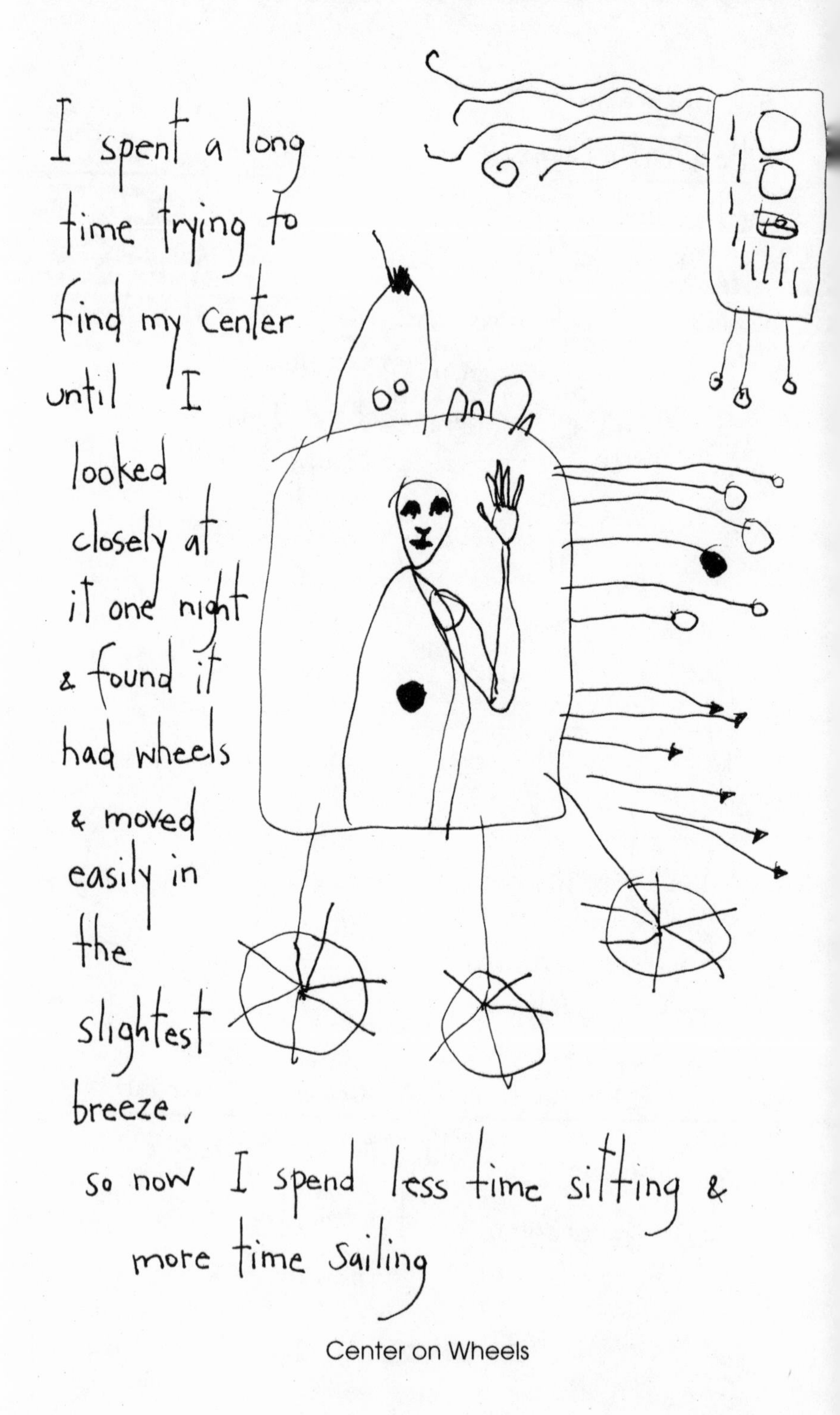

Center on Wheels

O no, she said, you
can't say just any
old thing to the Wind.
Only the Deepest
Secrets will do

& also you must
not use the letter i

The secret is
not in your
hand
    or your
    eye
        or your
        voice,
my aunt once
told me. The
secret is in
your heart.

Of course, she said, knowing
that doesn't make it any easier.

Illusion of Control

Hole in his Heart

She left pieces of her
life behind her
everywhere
she went.

It's easier
to feel the
sunlight
without them,
she said.

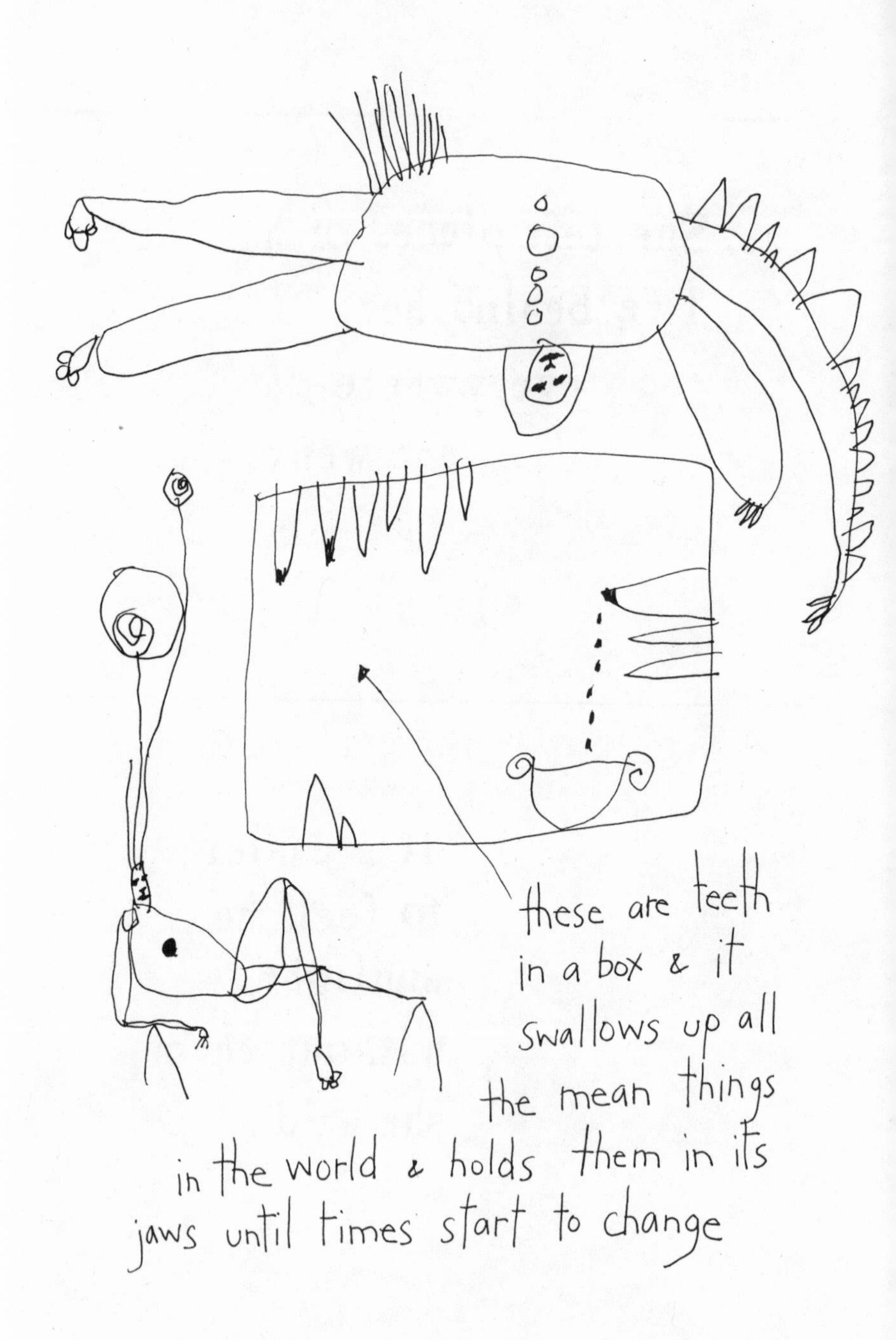

Teeth in a Box

My grandmother
used to say life
was so much
easier when you
were simple-minded.

It's taken me
almost my whole
life to understand
what she meant.

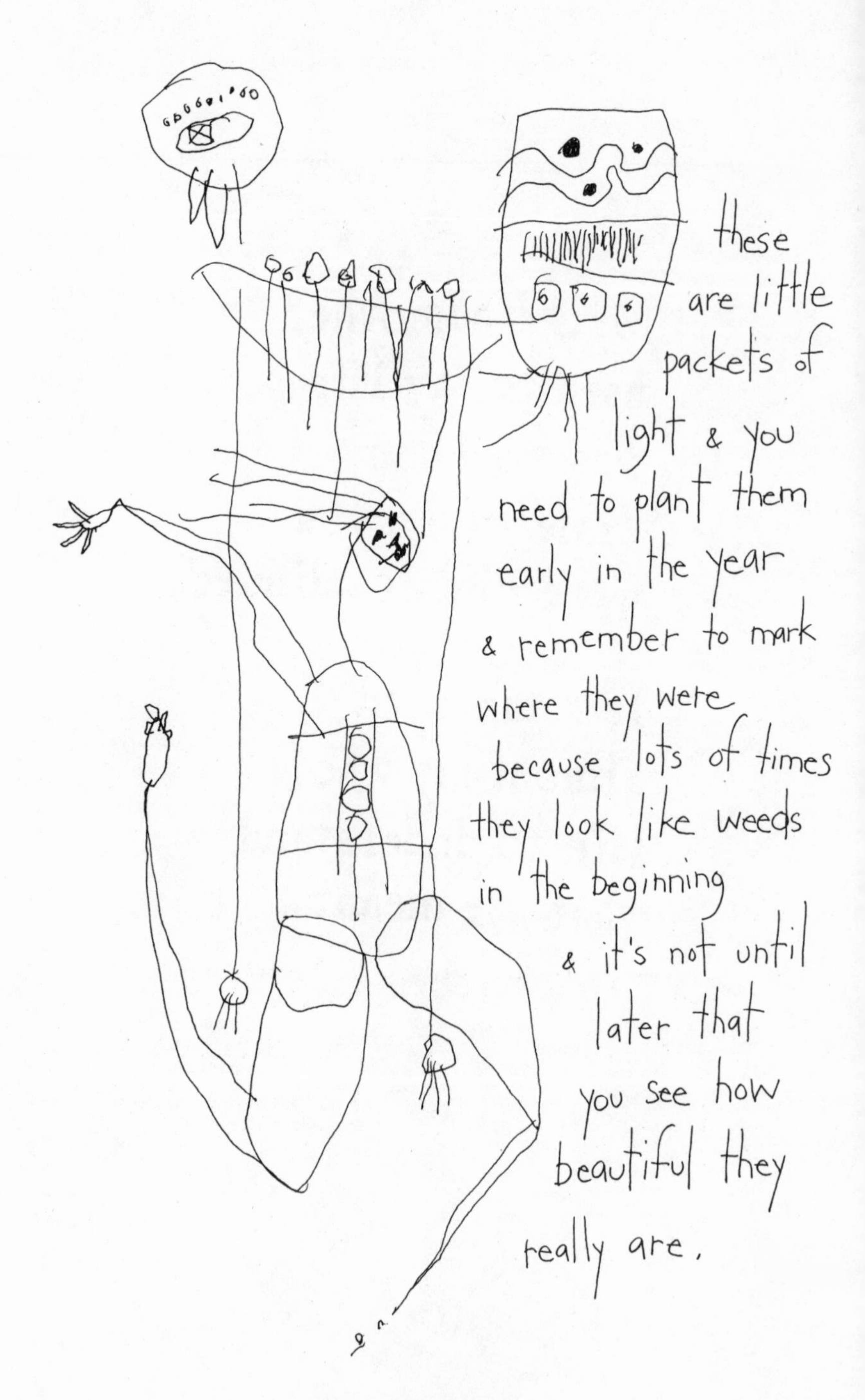

Packets of Light

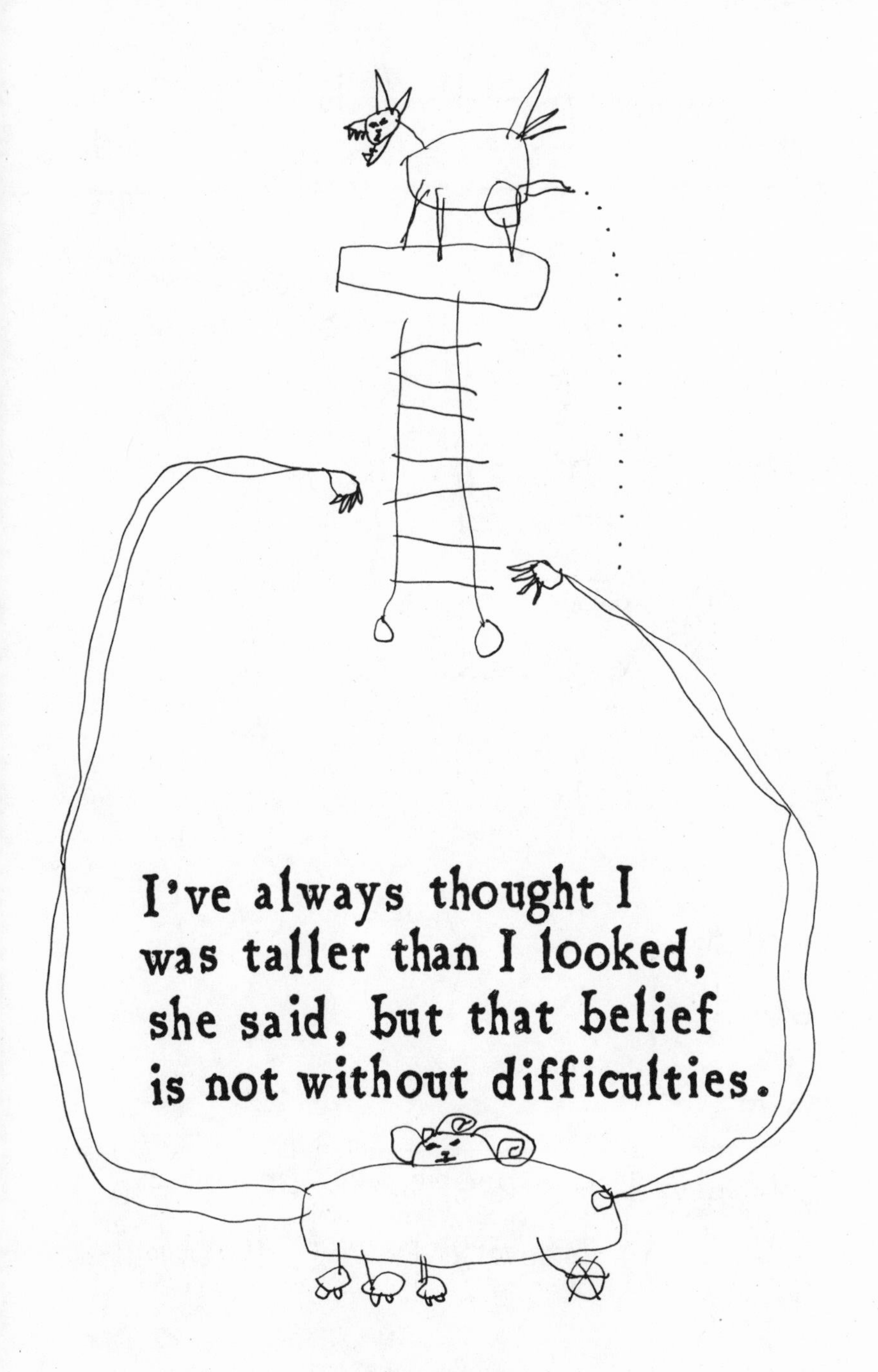

Believing Tall

There are 7 levels of hell, she said,

&

I think one of them is reserved for people who bring jello salads to every potluck they go to.

Jello Salad

Knowing Right

this is a giraffe bringing a
hostess gift of
juicy leaf
pizza because
he is so
tired of
there
never
being
anything
he can
eat at
these
functions

Leafy Pizza

It's not so
bad if you
don't think
of it as pizza,
she said. Just
think of it as
another one of
Mom's scary
hot dishes.

Death take me now &
spare me the pain, she
said. It was difficult
for me to get that
excited. Get a
grip, I said, it's
only aerobics.

Aerobics

Every afternoon my grandmother would have 2 chocolates with her coffee. I asked her once how many she thought she had eaten in her life. If you laid them all end to end to the moon & back, she said, I'd be sitting right here even as we speak

& then we celebrated her return with an extra chocolate.

Dancing Mailman

What's that thing?. I said.

O, that's an oar, he said,
in case we hit a calm
stretch & we decide we
need more excitement

& also it's good for
slapping sharks.

the next time the demons come, he SAid,
just wave your penis at
them. I can't do
that, I said.

Why not?
he said.

Well, I said finally.
because I'm American.

True American

There are times
I think I'm doing
things on principle,
but mostly I just
do what feels
good.

But that's a
principle, too.

Of course I believe
in heaven, my grandma
used to say.

There's got to be
some reward for
living with your
grandfather all
these years.

Early on, I resigned myself
to being in the dark
on all but the
most important
things,
she
said,
& it's not such a bad thing
because you don't see a lot of
the stuff you usually get anxious about.

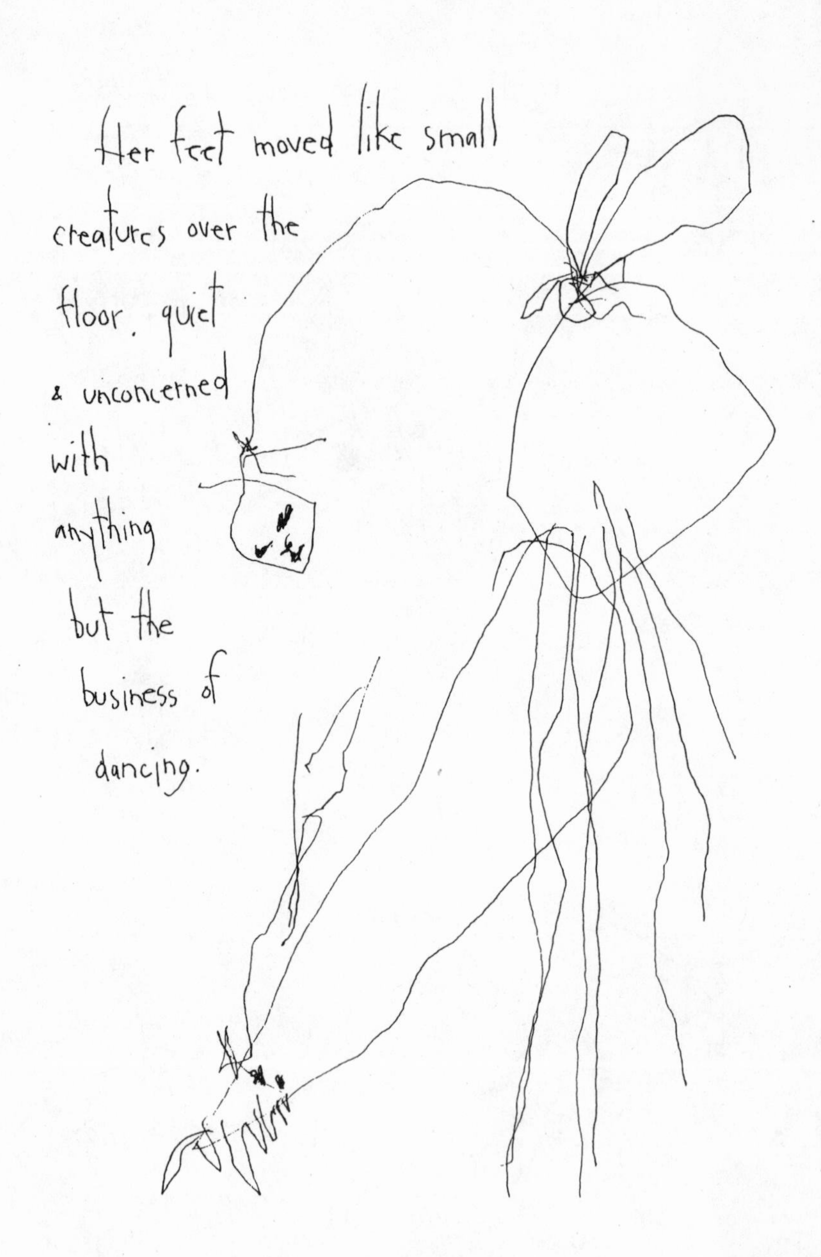
Her feet moved like small
creatures over the
floor, quiet
& unconcerned
with
anything
but the
business of
dancing.

Quiet Dance

they came to sit
& dangle their
feet off the edge
of the world

& after awhile
they forgot
everything but
the good & true
things they would
do someday

Angel of Dreams

My grandmother
told me once
that a city has
enough windows
for everybody.

I still want to believe her.

Don't you hear it? she
asked & I shook my head
no & then she started to
dance & suddenly there
was music everywhere &
it went on for a very long
time & when I finally
found words all I could
say was thank you.

He told me that the
night his mother died,
there were storms &
far away he saw purple
lightning & someone
left the window open
& the room filled
with a swirl of
butterflies & she
slipped out quietly
without anyone noticing

& I'm sure the grief was
softer because of that.

The birds
brought seeds
& flowers & bits
of brightly colored
string & placed them in
her hair while she slept so
that she would remember
the wild joy of
spring
when she
finally
awoke.

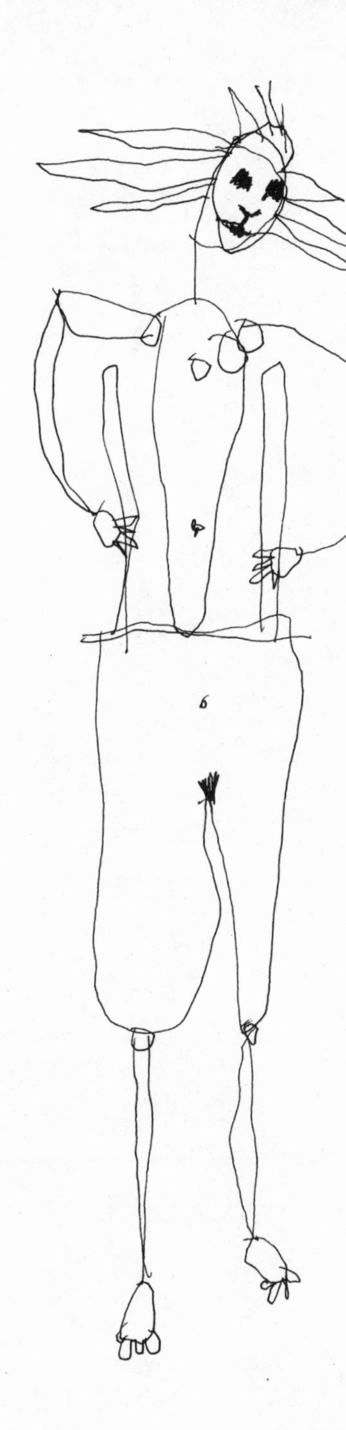

She tried on every
body left but they'd
been pretty well picked
over & all that were
left were a little
worse for wear.
She finally settled
on one that was
pretty good except
for a scuff at the
elbow where you
almost couldn't see
it anyway & as she
walked out into the
world she remembered
thinking next time
I'm going to get here
earlier.

Body Shop

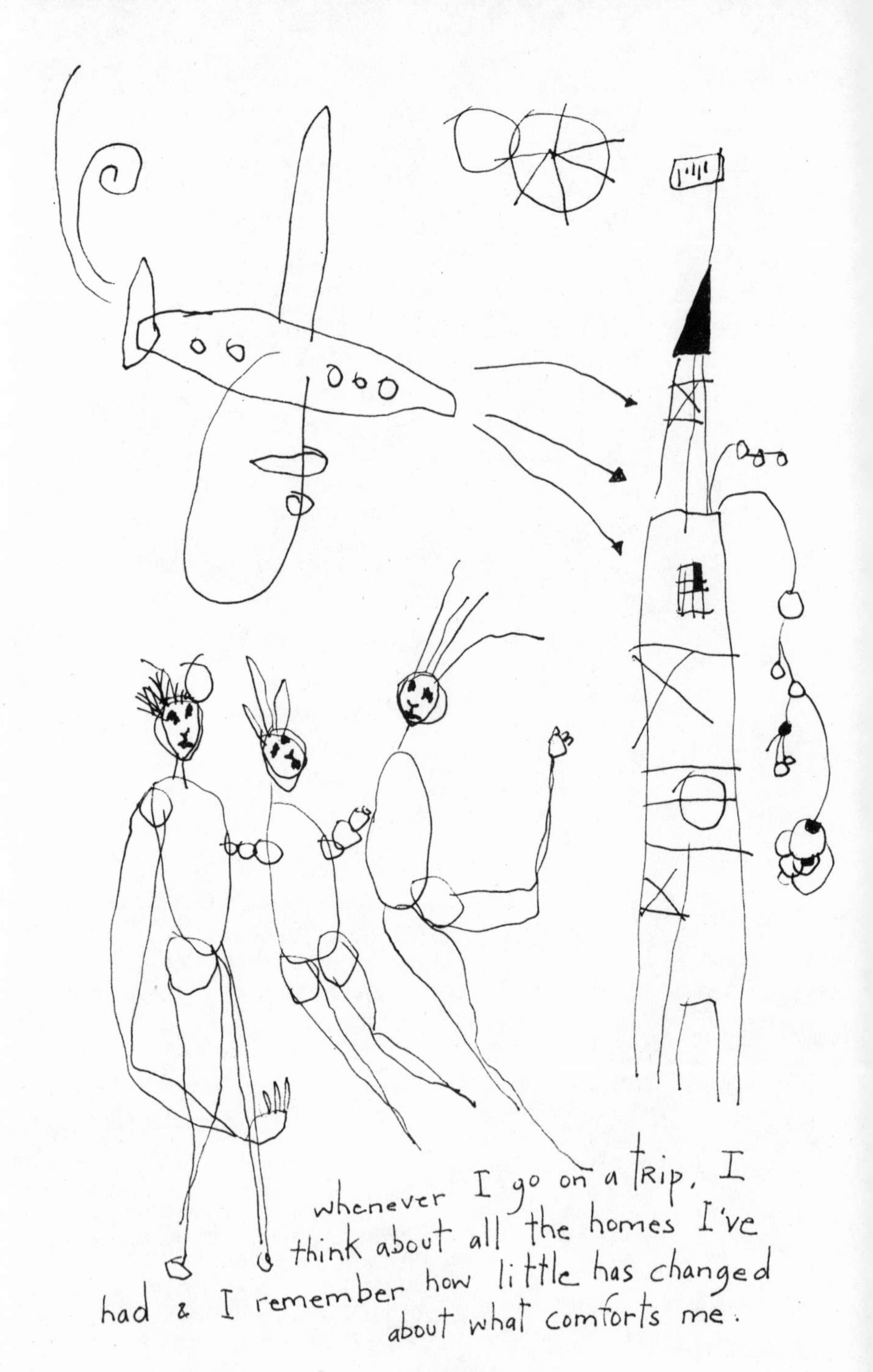
whenever I go on a trip, I
think about all the homes I've
had & I remember how little has changed
about what comforts me.

Comfort

I buried a nickel under the
porch when I was 8, she said,
but one day my grandma died
& they sold the house & I
never got to go back for it.

A nickel used to mean
something, I said.

She nodded. It still does,
she said & then she started
to cry.

Value of a Nickel

As long as the sun shall
rise goes the old lover's
vow. But we are children
of a scientific age & have
no time for poetry. Still,
I offer a quiet prayer of
thanks for the sunlight
each time I see your face.

When she wore the hat,
even many years later,
she could always smell
her mother's perfume

& it was hard
to remember
she was
supposed to
be alone.

Scent

There are days
I drop words
of comfort on
myself like
falling
leaves
& remember
that it is
enough to be
taken care of
by my self.

for a long
time, she
flew only
when she
thought
no one
else was
watching

I moved a lot
when I was
young & I still
ache a bit at
the thought of
all those
autumns in new
& unfamiliar
landscapes.

After his father
died, he carried
his life more
gently & left an
empty space
for the birds
& other creatures.

How old do you have
to be to die? he said
& I said I didn't
think anybody was
ever old enough

& that made sense
to him since he
was still new to
the world &
remembered how
forever had been.

Forever

every time I
looked at the
picture I
thought how I
should have
kissed her, so
finally I hid it
in the attic

& I wonder
if it's still there
with us both so
young & her
waiting to be
kissed

There are your fog
people & your sun
people, he said. I
said I wasn't sure
which kind I was.
He nodded. Fog'll
do that to you, he
said.

Meeting the Devil

I tried for a whole summer to teach our cat to play the piano. We started with an easy song. It was 3 Blind Mice. My dad said it didn't work because the cat had a tin ear, but I think it was because she kept looking around for the blind mice the whole time & never gave it her full attention.

Three Blind Mice

He won the grand
prize of a vacuum
cleaner & all the
canned goods he
could carry &
when they told him
he couldn't believe
it.

I thought I was
buying drink tickets,
he said.

Winning Ticket

Ghosts of the Past

A few said they'd be
horses. Most said they'd
be some sort of cat.
My friend said she'd
like to come back as a
porcupine.

I don't like crowds,
she said.

Every day he stood in
front of the Bank of
America. You're
trapped
in the belly
of a big
pink pig,
he said.

We ignored him.
We had work to do.

Belly of the Pig

Sleeping Man

She kept asking if the
stories were true. I kept
asking her if it mattered.

We finally gave up.'

She was looking for a
place to stand

& I wanted a place
to fly.

She told me
once that the
year she went
to England
she painted
all her buttons
yellow so
she would
remember
what the
sun felt like.

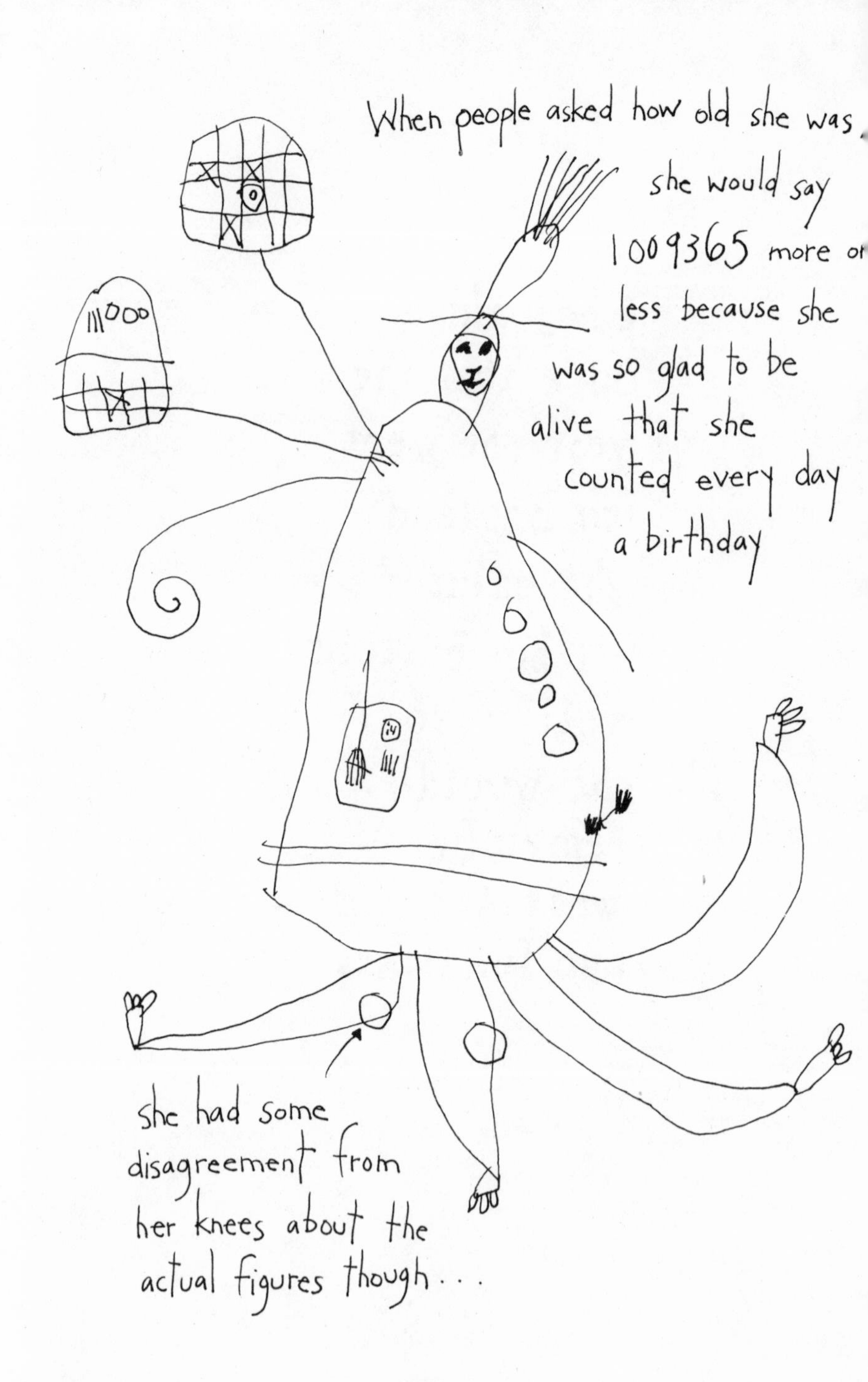
When people asked how old she was,
she would say
1009365 more or
less because she
was so glad to be
alive that she
counted every day
a birthday
she had some
disagreement from
her knees about the
actual figures though...

Birthdays

She told me she
moved to LA so
she could dye her
hair & be in a band.
A couple of years
after that someone
told me she'd quit
her band to go to
cosmetology school.
I guess it was easier
to give up music than
to give up the hair.

L.A. Hair

this is a pretty deep
hole for putting away all
the ugly things in the world.
For a long time it was empty,
but it started filling up
really fast the last couple
of years.

Deep Hole

I never
trusted
her for a
minute,
she said.
Her purse
was way
too big.

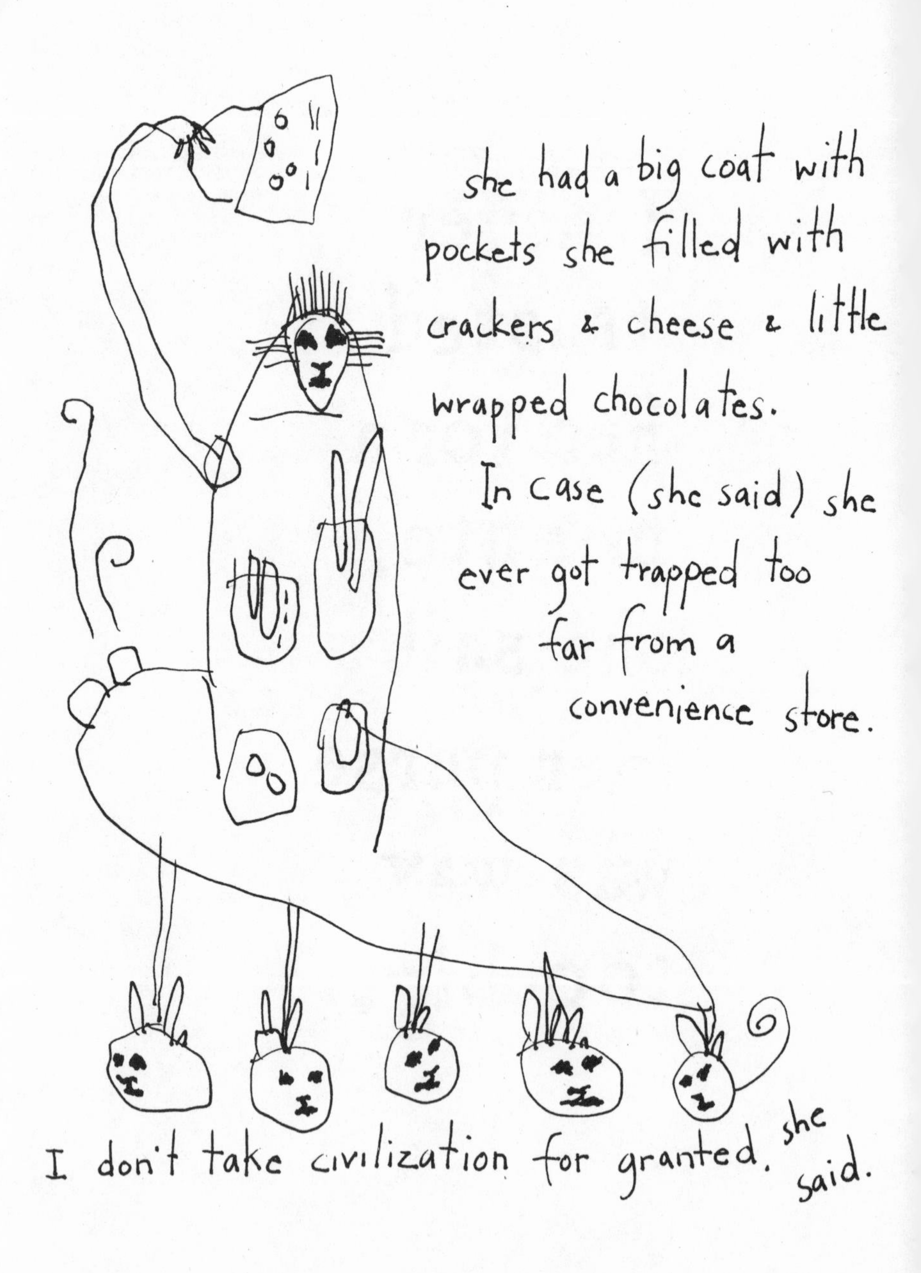
she had a big coat with
pockets she filled with
crackers & cheese & little
wrapped chocolates.
In case (she said) she
ever got trapped too
far from a
convenience store.
I don't take civilization for granted, she said.

Pockets

I don't
really have
any secrets,
she told
me once.
I just
forget
a lot of
stuff.

I thought, I'll
remove my head
for a while & it
went fine except
most people didn't
know where to
look when we
were having a
conversation.

she always
camouflaged
herself as
a crowd.
I've never
been lonely,
she said,
but sometimes
it's hard to
think above
the noise.

Crowd

I was never good at hide
& seek because I'd always
make enough noise so my
friends would be sure to
find me. I don't have
anyone to play those games
with any more, but now &
then I make enough noise
just in case someone is
still looking & hasn't
found me yet.

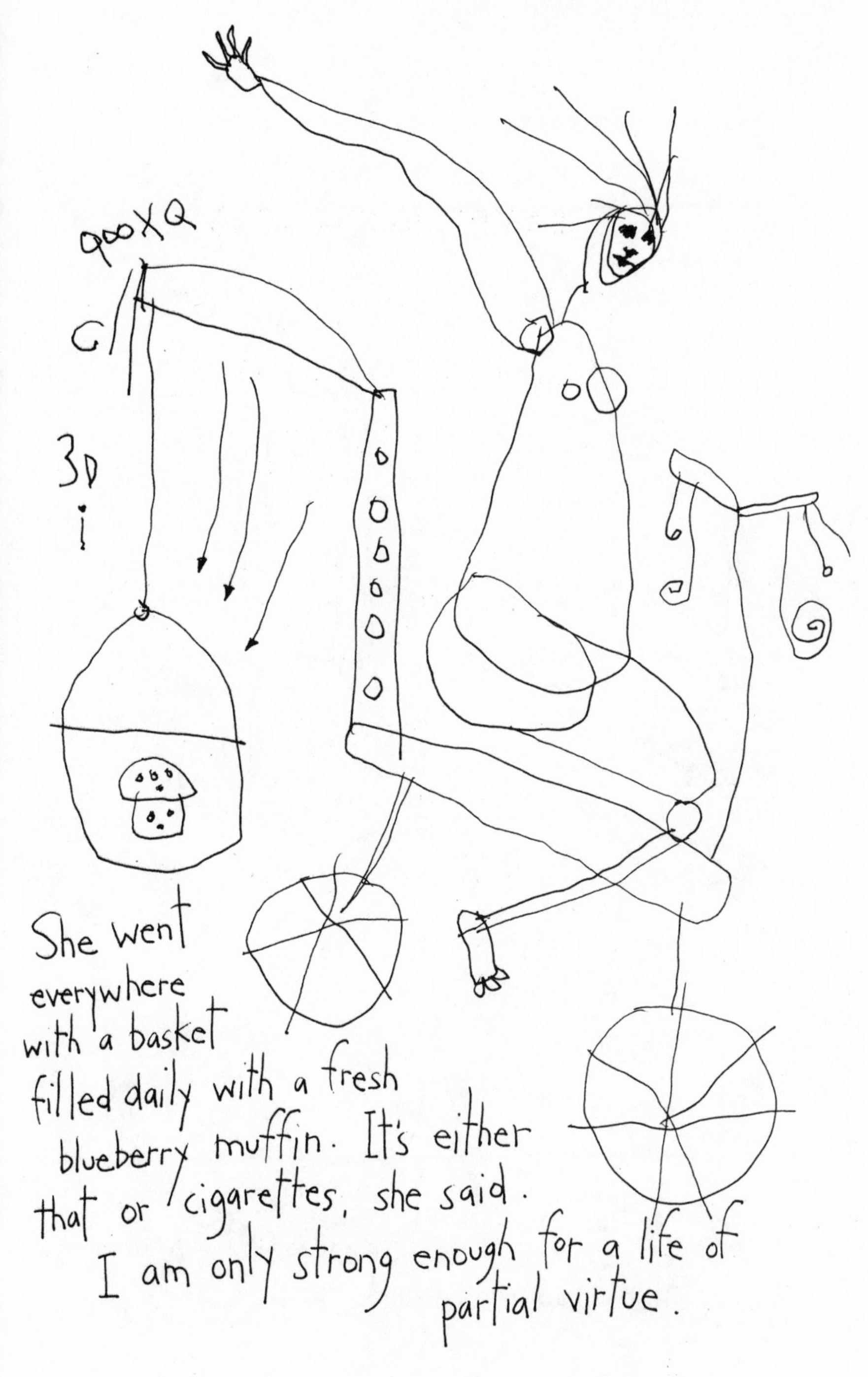

Partial Virtue

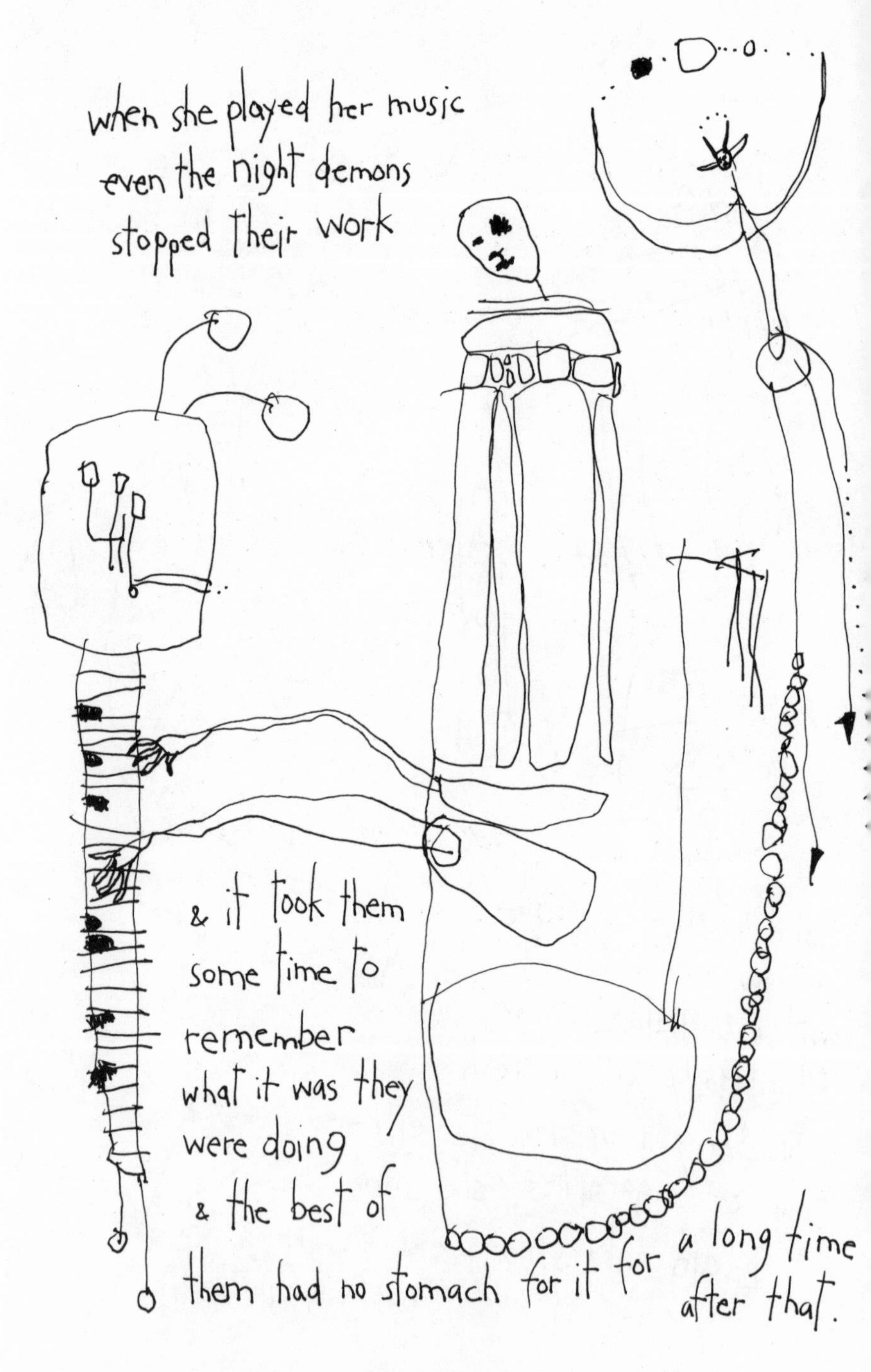

Night Demons

The plumber was digging around
in the pipes & he saw something
shine in the muck & it turned
out to be the soul of the last
tenant.

He gave it to me & I said I
wonder how we can return it &
he shrugged & said he found
stuff like that all the time.

You'd be amazed what people
lose, he said.

The elephant head
was the most unusual
piece in her wardrobe
& even though she
never wore it in
public, it gave her
great comfort to
know she could if
she wanted to.

Classic Piece

most people don't
know there are
angels whose only
job is to make sure
you don't get too
comfortable & fall
asleep & miss your
life

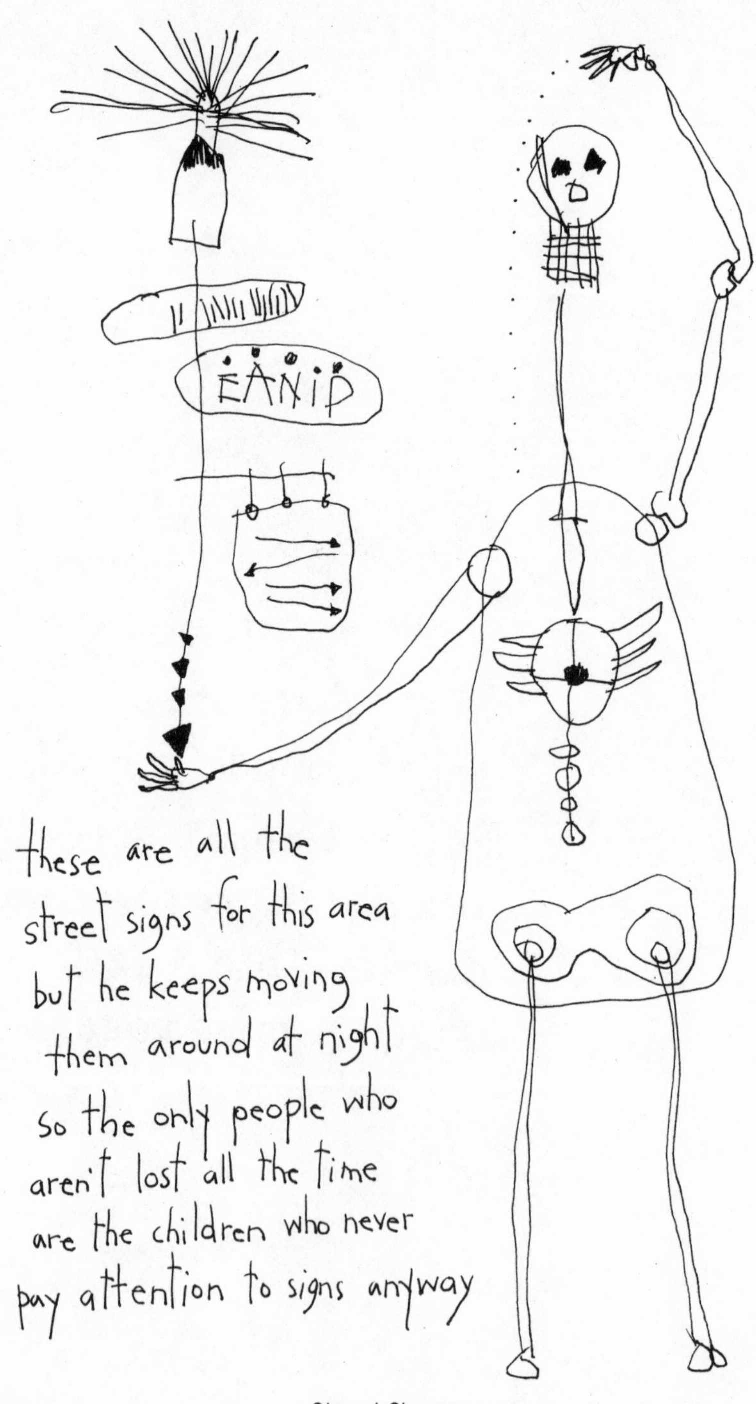

Street Signs

My great-aunt told
me once to remember
that old people need
bananas.

I remember.
Someday I will
tell my sons.

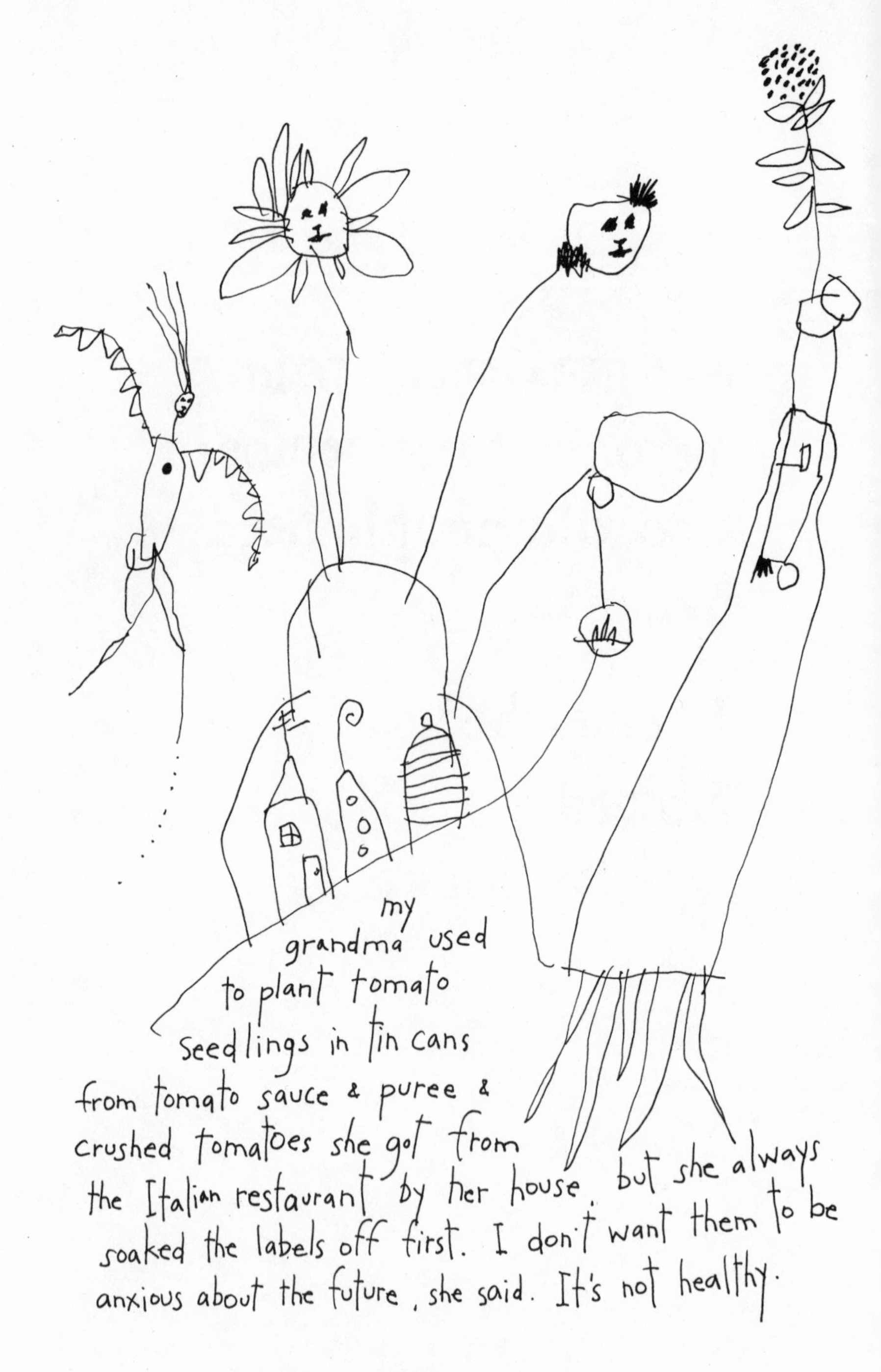

Young Tomatoes

There are lives I can
imagine without children

but none of them have
the same laughter
& noise.

my aunt
had a poodle
she dressed
in little red
sweaters with
little dangly
ball things
& I don't think it was any wonder that
dog was so vicious.

Attack Dog

After he was quiet
a long time, words
began to come to
him in dreams &
told him their
secret names & this
was the way he learned
the true nature of
the world.

Too Much Stuff

He told me that once
he forgot himself & his
heart opened up like a
door with a loose latch
& everything fell out &
he tried for days to put
it all back in the proper
order, but finally he
gave up & left it there
in a pile & loved
everything equally.

My grandmother was big & solid. My grandfather was tall & thin. They looked an unlikely couple.

I asked them once how they ended up together. My grandmother said she won him fair & square in an arm wrestling match.

My grandpa just smiled. I let you win, he said.

we had gone
far enough
together to
listen easily
in the quiet
spaces

The day he first told me he was starting to disappear I didn't believe him & so he stopped & held his hand up to the sun & it was like thin paper in the light & finally I said. you seem very calm for a man who is disappearing & he said it was a relief after all those years of trying to keep the pieces of his life in one place. Later on, I went to see him again & as I was leaving, he put a package in my hand.

This is the last piece of my life. he said. take good care of it & then he smiled & was gone & the room filled with the sound of the wind & when I opened the package there was nothing there & I thought there must be some mistake or maybe I dropped it & I

got down on my hands &
knees & looked until the light
began to fade & then slowly
I felt pieces of my life
fall away & suddenly I
understood what he meant
& I lay there for a long
time crying & laughing at
the same time.

I don't
mind being
a temp,
she told me.

It reminds
me of my
priorities.

Temp

Older doesn't
always mean
wiser, my
grandfather
once said.
Sometimes
it just means
older.

She said she usually
cried at least once
each day not because
she was sad, but
because the world was
so beautiful & life
was so short.

Ten Commandments

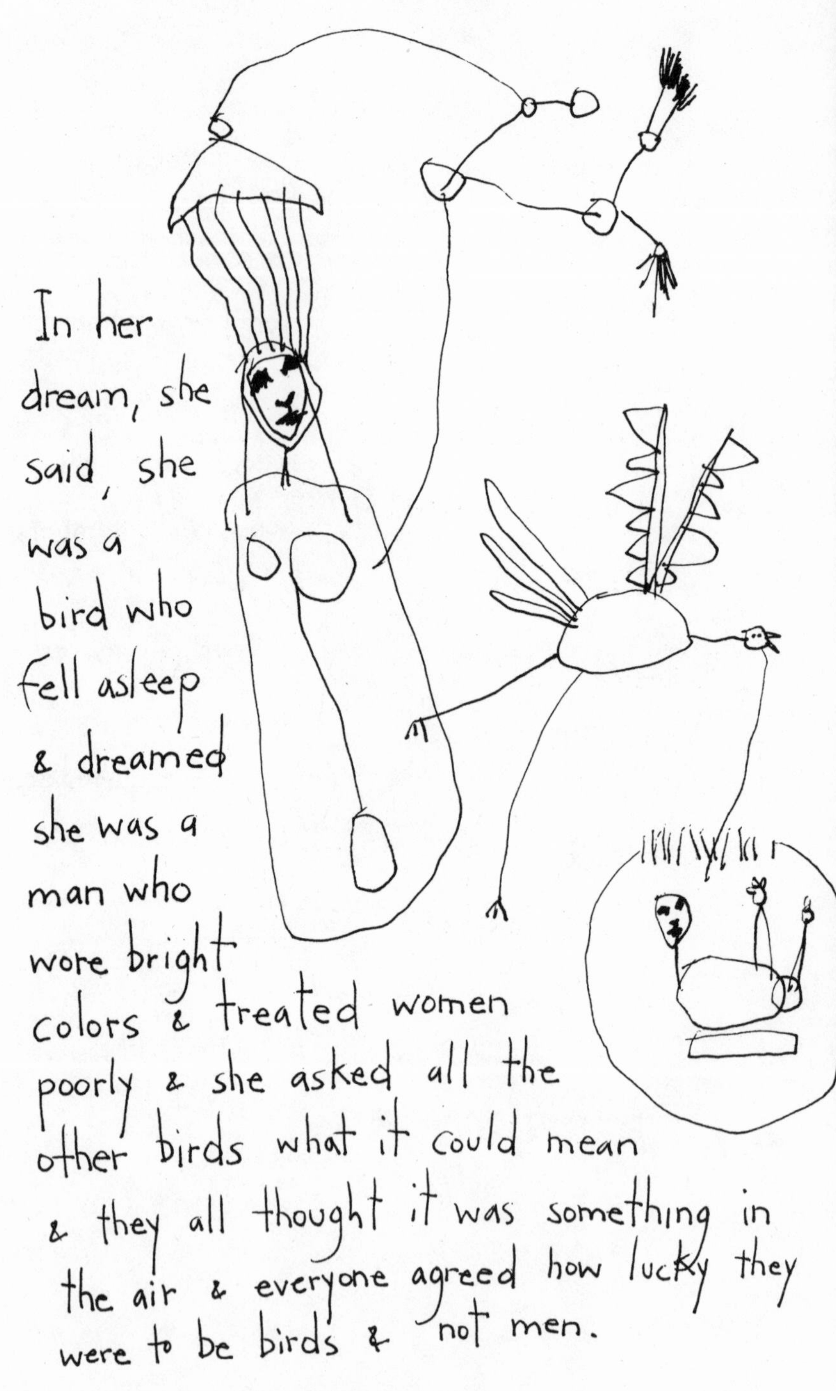
In her
dream, she
said, she
was a
bird who
fell asleep
& dreamed
she was a
man who
wore bright
colors & treated women
poorly & she asked all the
other birds what it could mean
& they all thought it was something in
the air & everyone agreed how lucky they
were to be birds & not men.

Bird Dreams

I once had a garden
filled with flowers
that grew only on dark
thoughts

but they need constant
attention

& one day I decided
I had better things
to do.

The preacher dunked her head 3 times in the basin & called out for the demons to leave & then she spit water in his face.

So he extemporaneously added a fourth & by the time she came up for air the demons were considerably more restrained.

One time on Hollywood
Boulevard I saw a young girl
with a baby. It was a crisp
winter morning & her hair
shone dark purple in the sun.
She was panhandling outside
the Holiday Inn & the door
clerk came out & told her
to be on her way & I
remember thinking that
purple seemed like a good
color for a madonna, so
I gave her a dollar just
in case.

My grandpa used to tell
us about a man who had
3 heads who lived in his
town & he was always in
the kitchen frying something
or other & even though it
smelled like chicken it was
really the bones of children.
He was awake every time
I saw him, my grandpa
said, even late at night &
we decided maybe he had
3 or 4 jobs but that's what
you need with so many
mouths to feed & then
my grandma would make us
come in & watch educational
television for our own good.

We lay there & looked up at
the night sky & she told me
about stars called blue squares
& red swirls & I told her I'd
never heard of them.

Of course not, she said,
the really important stuff they
never tell you. You have to
imagine it on your own.

we used to go visit my
grandma on the train &
on the way my sister & I
would talk to people we
met & tell them we were
from Hawaii & could speak
Polynesian & I'd hold up a
7-Up & say this is called
puka-puka-wanini on the
Big Island & we'd make up
longer & longer names until
it took about 10 minutes
to say one & about that time
we would be there & we'd
say aloha & go off to have
lunch at my grandma's &
my sister would hold up a
Mrs. Paul's fish stick & say
in Hawaii they call these
molo-molo-pooey-pooey &
I'd try not to choke on
my fruit punch.

Native Hawaiians

When I first discovered the moon, he said, I gave it a different name. But everyone kept calling it the moon. The real name never caught on.

Your cat seems very
healthy, I said to her.

That is not a cat, she
said. That is a pig in
cat's clothing.

we
don't
have much
time, he said,
so I'll just
tell you about me.

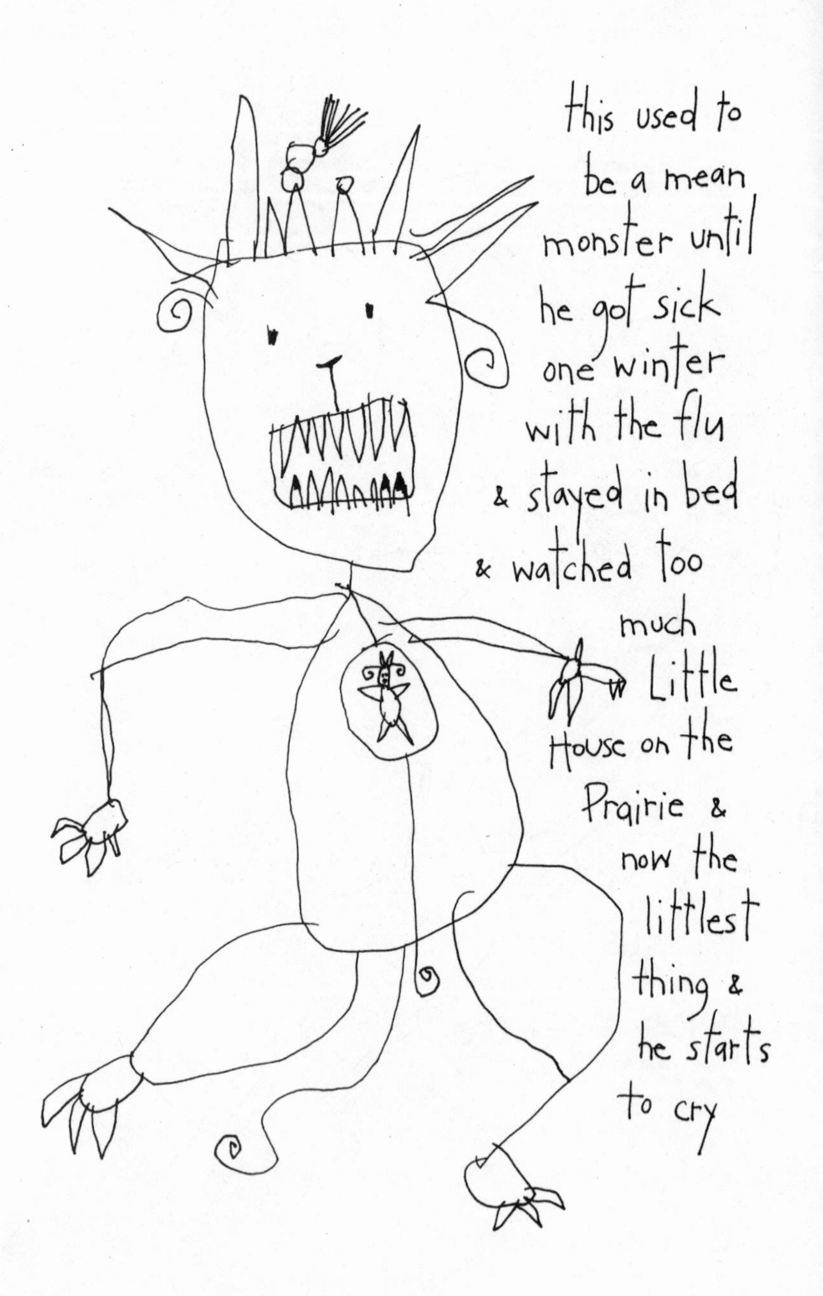
this used to
be a mean
monster until
he got sick
one winter
with the flu
& stayed in bed
& watched too
much
Little
House on the
Prairie &
now the
littlest
thing &
he starts
to cry

He told me once
that if I kept it
up long enough
I'd probably get
wise enough to
be silly in public,

but I probably
won't wait
that long.

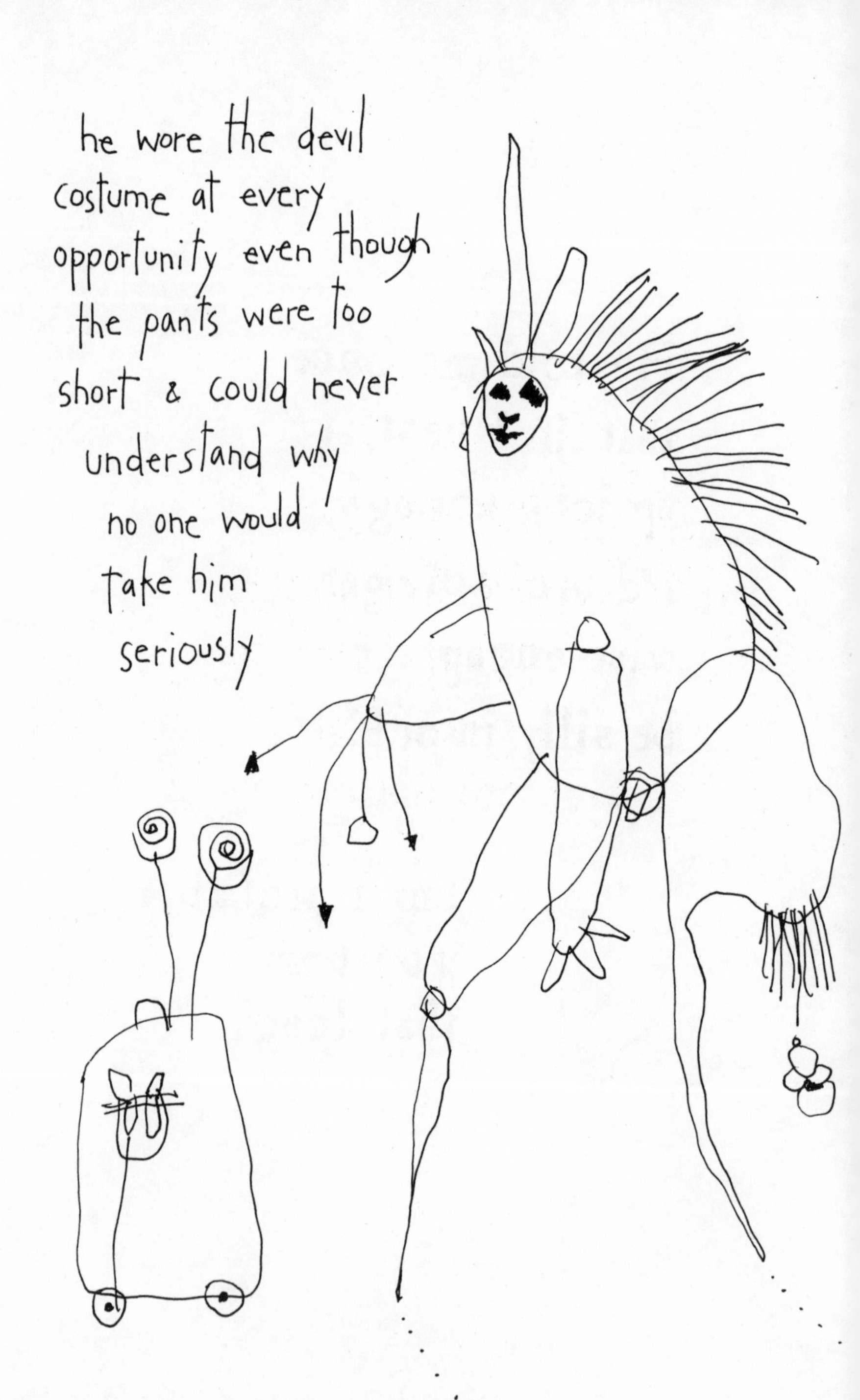
he wore the devil
costume at every
opportunity even though
the pants were too
short & could never
understand why
no one would
take him
seriously

Short Pants

He told me the best
way to make coffee
was to add an egg,
so I did & he looked
at the strands floating
in his cup & decided
to have tea instead.

Egg Coffee

I don't know if I really believe in all the saints, she said, but I pray to them anyway.

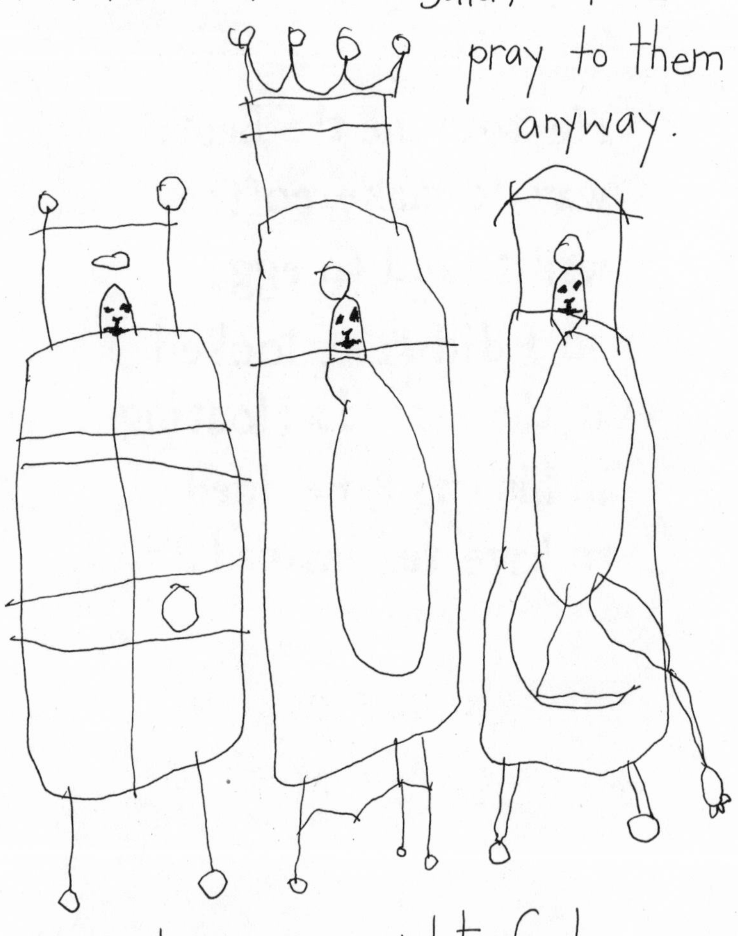

It makes every night feel more like a slumber party.

Slumber Party

The first time
I played golf,
I had the most
fun throwing
bread to the
goldfish in the
pro shop. It
made as much
sense as anything
else.

Wheelbarrow

I used to wait for a sign, she said, before I did anything. Then one night I had a dream & an angel in black tights came to me & said, You can start any time now & then I asked is this a sign? & the angel started laughing & I woke up.

Now, I think the whole world is filled with signs, but if there's no laughter, I know they're not for me.

Waiting for Signs

She seemed to
move everywhere
dancing & music
followed her

like

leaves

on

the

wind.

Are you a princess?
I said & she said I'm
much more than a
princess

but you don't have
a name for it yet
here on earth.

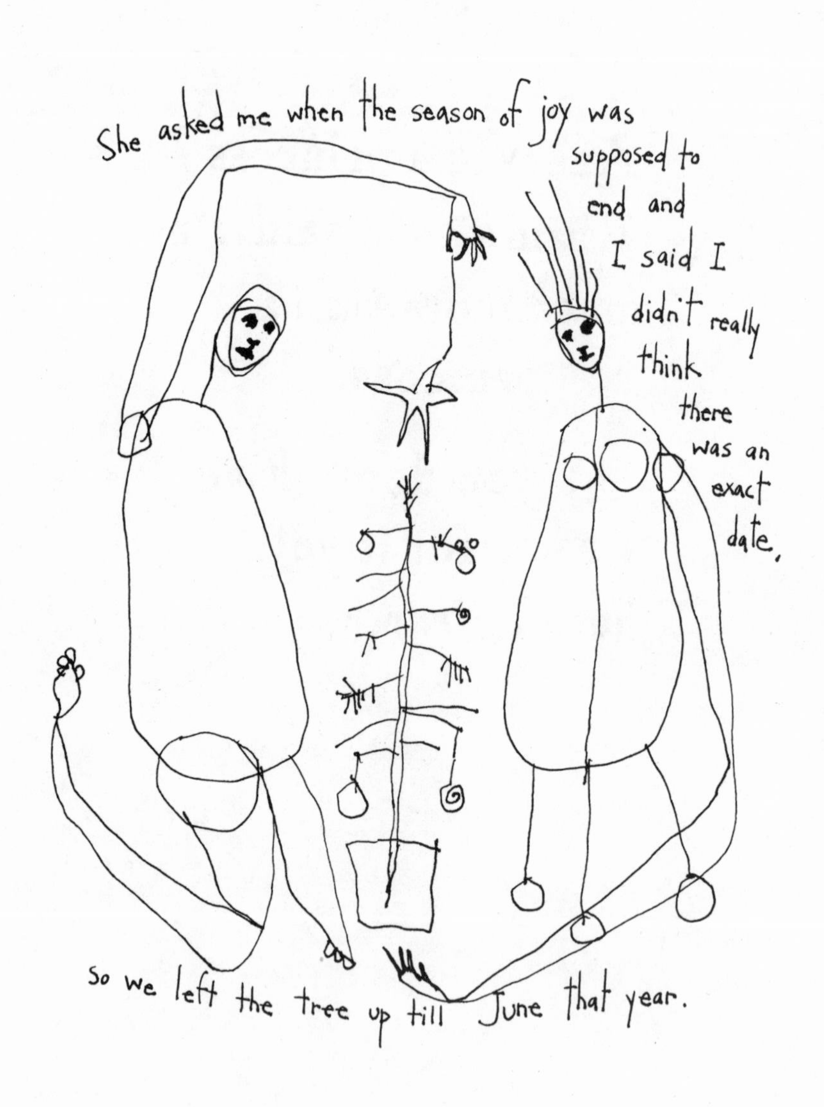

Season of Joy

When I met the
Grandfather of
Time, he said
it was no use
struggling.

Even after all
these years he
still had too
much to do.

The clock is a conspiracy
& a crime against humanity

& I would not
own one

except I miss
appointments
without it.

Make sure you got
clean underwear, she
always said, in case
you get in an accident
& I always figured
that'd be the least
of my worries, but
now I'm older & I
see there's a lot you
can't control & some
you can control &
clean underwear is
one of those you can.

for the most part

I have too much to lose,
she said, if I cross that
line.

Like what? I said. She
could not think of
anything that day so she
said she'd get back to me.

Since then I've been
thinking what I would
lose if I crossed my
line & I haven't come
up with anything either.

There's always another
line somewhere.

It was a summer's
night & the smell
of the old rose bush
was as heavy as rain
& she asked me in

& I followed her
up those stairs till
morning.

Summer's Night

Self-Conscious

If I was a spider princess,
she said, I would spin
webs the color of sky &
catch drops of sunlight
to give to children who
watch too much tv & then
everyone would remember
to come outside to play.

If I was a spider
princess, she said,
things would be
different.

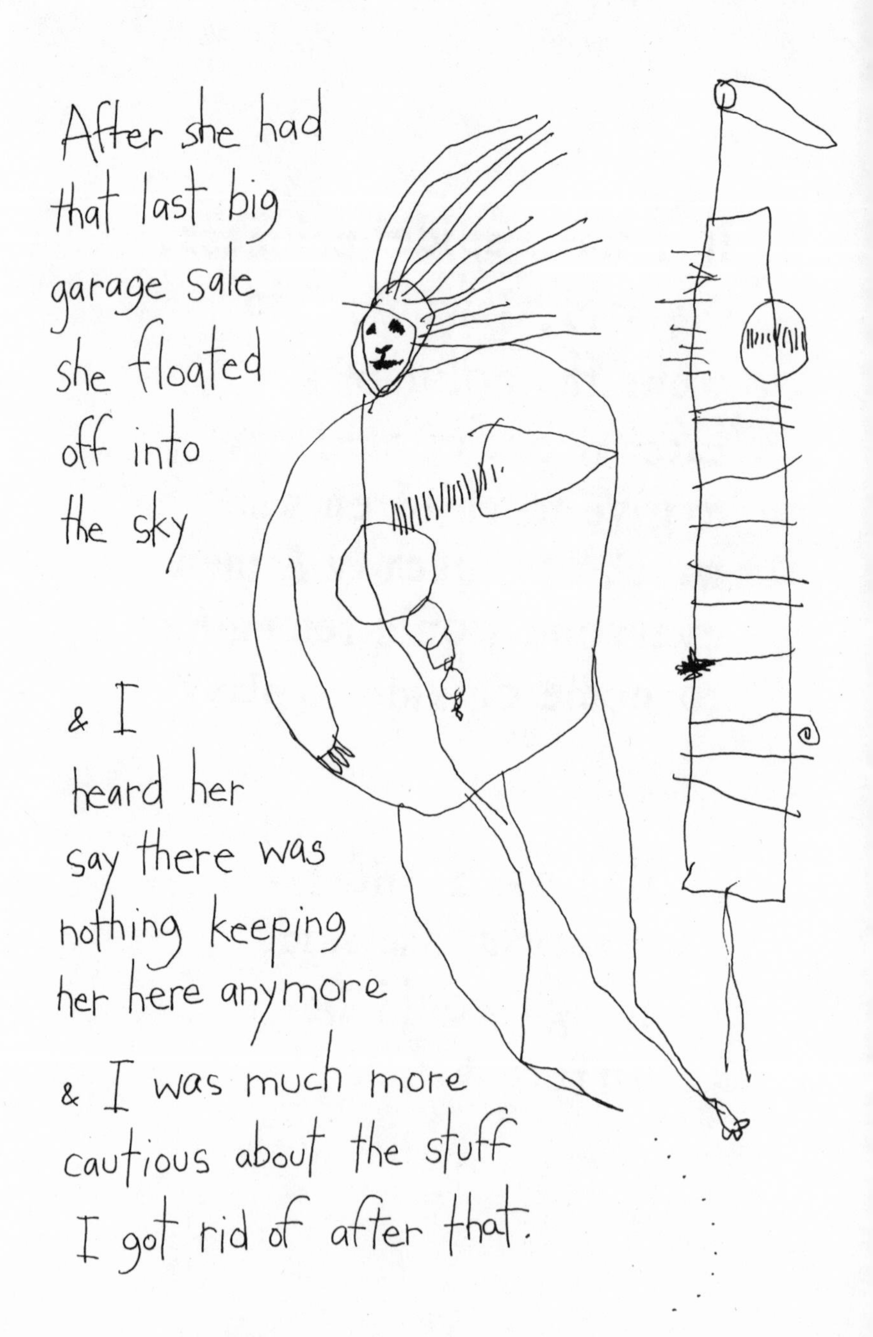
After she had
that last big
garage sale
she floated
off into
the sky
& I
heard her
say there was
nothing keeping
her here anymore
& I was much more
cautious about the stuff
I got rid of after that.

Garage Sale

I was waiting for the
longest time, she said.
I thought you forgot.

It is hard to forget, I
said, when there is
such an empty space
when you are gone.

When I was young I told everyone I had a twin sister. One day, after we had been to see the relatives, my mother told me I was too old to play that game any more. So I stopped talking about her & after awhile, she finally went away.

But I'm grown up now & I still miss her & I wish she would come back.

The first time her laughter
unfurled its wings in the wind,
we knew that the world would
never be the same.

I've always liked living in the past best, she said.

It takes less money than I make now.

She saw herself
reflected in the
store window &
then the sun
changed & she
disappeared &
all she could
see was her eyes
& she remembered
thinking, I make
a very nice floor
lamp & that was
the day she decided
to quit her job.

Epiphany

There was a single blue
line of crayon drawn across
every wall in the house.
What does it mean? I asked.
A pirate needs the sight of
the sea, he said & then he
pulled his eye patch down
& turned & sailed away.

Crayon Pirate

he said the hat
kept his soul from
drifting off & I
asked if he knew
this from experience
& he laughed &
said all his best
bits were from
National Geographic

National Geographic Hat

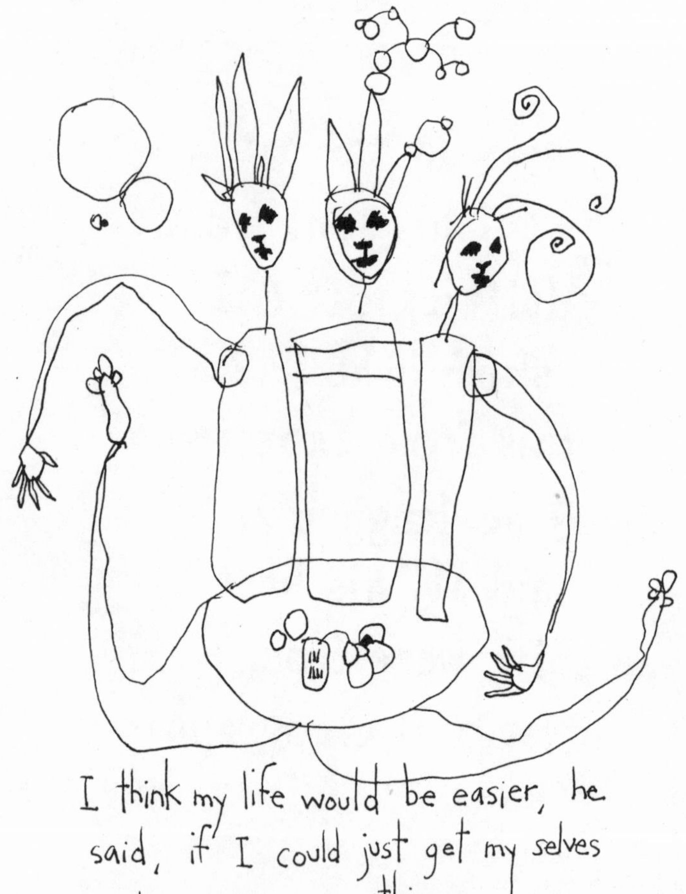

I think my life would be easier, he said, if I could just get my selves to agree on something.

Selves to Agree

In my dream,
the angel shrugged
& said, If we
fail this time, it
will be a failure of
imagination

& then she placed the world
gently in the palm of my hand.

About the Artist

Brian Andreas is a fiber artist, sculptor, and storyteller. He uses traditional media from fine art, theatre and storytelling, as well as computer networks and multimedia to explore new forms of human community. He also likes to make art with the rustiest stuff he can find. His work is shown and collected internationally.

Though he holds a B.A. from Luther College, and an M.F.A. in Fiber and Mixed Media from John F. Kennedy University, the majority of his education has come from his wife, Ellen, & their two children.

After years of adventure on the West Coast of the United States, he now lives with his family in Iowa, where he writes most of his new stories on little white restaurant napkins you find in roadside diners everywhere.

Index of Stories

More Than a Princess	*Mostly True*
National Geographic Hat	*Mostly True*
Native Hawaiians	*Still Mostly True*
Neighbors	*Going Somewhere Soon*
Night Demons	*Still Mostly True*
No More Secret	*Still Mostly True*
Odd Couple	*Mostly True*
Open Heart	*Going Somewhere Soon*
Opera Man	*Going Somewhere Soon*
Packets of Light	*Going Somewhere Soon*
Partial Virtue	*Still Mostly True*
Pig Cat	*Mostly True*
Place to Fly	*Mostly True*
Pockets	*Mostly True*
Porcupine	*Mostly True*
Preacher & the Demons	*Still Mostly True*
Presence of Mind	*Mostly True*
Principles	*Going Somewhere Soon*
Purple Madonna	*Going Somewhere Soon*
Quiet Dance	*Going Somewhere Soon*
Quiet Prayer	*Still Mostly True*
Quiet Spaces	*Still Mostly True*
Remembering	*Still Mostly True*
Roughage	*Going Somewhere Soon*
Running Behind	*Still Mostly True*
Scent	*Going Somewhere Soon*
Season of Joy	*Still Mostly True*
Secret Heart	*Still Mostly True*
Secret Names	*Still Mostly True*
Secret Notes	*Mostly True*
Self-Conscious	*Still Mostly True*
Selves to Agree	*Still Mostly True*
Short Pants	*Still Mostly True*
Silly in Public	*Still Mostly True*
Simple Mind	*Still Mostly True*
Slapping Sharks	*Mostly True*
Sleeping Man	*Mostly True*
Slumber Party	*Going Somewhere Soon*
Songs to Herself	*Mostly True*
Spider Princess	*Still Mostly True*
Street Signs	*Still Mostly True*

Index of StoryPeople Galleries

ALABAMA
Clary-Sage, Birmingham
Ashland Gallery, Mobile
Wall Decor, Orange Beach

ALASKA
Artique, Ltd., Anchorage

ARIZONA
Mind's Eye, Scottsdale
Pink Adobe Galleries, Tuscon

ARKANSAS
The Heights Gallery, Little Rock

CALIFORNIA
Studio Gallery, Alameda
ZIA Houseworks, Berkeley
The Artful Eye, Calistoga
What Iz Art, Cambria
Bella Cosa, Claremont
Meadowlark, Corte Madera
Fire & Rain, Folsom
The Artful Eye, Healdsburg
Copperfield's, Hesperia
Los Gatos Company, Los Gatos
Icaan Galleries, Manhattan Beach
Coda Gallery, Palm Desert
Spirals, Palo Alto
Del Mano, Pasadena
Occasions, Riverside
Fire & Rain, Sacramento
Connections for Design, San Carlos
Twigg St. Gallery, San Diego
17 Reasons, San Francisco
Cedanna, San Francisco
SMILE Gallery, San Francisco
Yerba Buena Center, San Francisco
Hands Gallery, San Luis Obispo
Paula Best Gallery, San Martin
Santa Barbara Art Co., Santa Barbara
The IMP, Santa Monica
Handmade, Sherman Oaks
Legends, Sonoma
Sassafras, Sonora
Fine Eye, Sutter Creek
Rubber Boots, Toluca Lake
Kitchen Table, Walnut Creek

COLORADO
Heather Gallery, Aspen
The Middle Fish, Boulder
Highlands Gallery, Breckenridge
Show of Hands, Denver
Caviano, Littleton

CONNECTICUT
The Spirited Hand, Avon
Evergreen, Guilford
Heron Gallery, Kent
WAVE Gallery, New Canaan
WAVE Gallery, New Haven
Clair de Lune, West Mystic

DELAWARE
Stone Heart, Rehoboth Beach

DIST. OF COLUMBIA
Cattin' Around, D.C.

FLORIDA
American Craftworks, Boca Raton
Island Style, Captiva Island
IBIS Gallery, Cedar Key
Nicholson House, Clearwater
The ZOO Gallery, Destin

Seldom Seen, Ft. Lauderdale
High Springs Gallery, High Springs
Brooke Pottery, Lakeland
Nicholson House, Orlando
Bayfront, Pensacola
The Purple House, Punta Gorda
Island Style, Sanibel Island
The Artful Dodger, Sarasota
Nomads Gallery, Tallahassee
Nicholson House, Tampa
Gallery Five, Tequesta
Timothy's, Winter Park

GEORGIA
Frontier, Athens
Bennett Street, Atlanta
Soho Gallery, Atlanta
Cody Road Workshops, Mt. Airy
The Hambidge Center, Rabin Gap

HAWAII
Contemporary Museum, Honolulu

IDAHO
Two Fishes Gallery, Ketchum

ILLINOIS
A Unique Presence, Chicago
Mindscape, Evanston
Poopsies, Galena
The Good Works Gallery, Glen Ellyn
Artisan's Shop, Long Grove
Paula's Gallery, Rockford
A Unique Presence, Skokie
Sue Thompson Gallery, Springfield
The Artisan's Shop, Wilmette

INDIANA
Wildflower, Evansville
Details, Indianapolis
F.B. Fogg, Muncie
The Mole Hole, South Bend

IOWA
Henry Myrtle Gallery, Cedar Falls
Artistic Accents, Cedar Rapids
Agora Arts, Decorah
Out of Hand, Des Moines
Iowa Artisans Gallery, Iowa City

KANSAS
M Taylor, Leawood & Prairie Village

KENTUCKY
Churchill Weavers, Berea
Sister Dragonfly, Louisville
Addie Lowe's Lagniappe, Paducah

LOUISIANA
Artifacts, New Orleans

MAINE
Abacus, Booth Bay Harbor
Abacus, Freeport
Plum Dandy, Kennebunkport
Abacus, Portland

MARYLAND
Nouveau Contemporary Goods, Baltimore
OXOXO Gallery, Baltimore
As Kindred Spirits, Rockville
The Mind's Eye, St. Michaels

MASSACHUSETTS
Monty's, Boston
Lacoste, Concord
Artique, Framingham
The Hand of Man, Lenox
Concetta's, Marblehead
Signature Gallery, Mashpee
Jubilation, Newton Centre
The Artisan Gallery, Northampton
Craftworks, Oak Bluffs
Square Circle, Rockport
Monty's, South Wellfleet

MICHIGAN
16 Hands, Ann Arbor
Art Loft, Birmingham

Art Folk, Grand Rapids
Coyote Woman, Harbor Springs
Uptown Gallery , Holland
Todd Mack Gallery, Lansing
Inland Passage, Leland
Northwood Gallery, Midland
Ariana, Royal Oak
Objects of Art, West Bloomfield

MINNESOTA
The Afternoon, Bloomington
Cornucopia, Lanesboro
The Bibelot Shops, Mpls/St. Paul
StoryPeople, Rochester
Good Things, White Bear Lake

MISSISSIPPI
Main Street Gallery, Starkville

MISSOURI
Blue Stem, Columbia

MONTANA
Latigo & Lace, Augusta
Seven Doors Down, Bozeman

NEBRASKA
University Place Art Center, Lincoln
The Afternoon, Omaha

NEVADA
Pipe Dreams, Reno

NEW HAMPSHIRE
Woodworker's Gallery, Milford
Sky i Gallery, Nashua
Gallery 33, Portsmouth

NEW JERSEY
Right Angle, Manalapan
Dexterity, Montclair
Go for Baroque, Princeton
Art Forms, Red Bank
American Pie, Stone Harbor
Eurica, Wyckoff

NEW MEXICO
Mariposa, Albuquerque
Copelands, Alamagordo
Jack of All Arts, Madrid
Off the Wall, Santa Fe

NEW YORK
The Eclectic Collector, Katonah
Wendy Gee!, Larchmont
Sweetheart Gallery Too, Woodstock
An American Craftsman, NYC
New York Public Library, NYC
Wares for Art, NYC
Creator's Hands Too, Rochester
The Creator's Hands, Rochester
Christopher Gallery, Stony Brook

NORTH CAROLINA
Budding Artists, Atlantic Beach
New Morning Gallery, Asheville
Starwood, Blowing Rock
The Bag Lady, Charlotte
Outer Banks Style, Corolla
The Davidson Icehouse, Davidson
Rag Poets Societe, Greensboro
Over the Moon, Ocracoke
Little Art Gallery, Raleigh
Urban Artware, Winston Salem
New Elements, Wilmington

NORTH DAKOTA
Boerth's, Fargo

OHIO
Drumm Studios, Akron
Angels & Other Folk, Chagrin Falls
Only Artists, Cincinnati
The Artworks, Findlay
Outlines, Youngstown

OKLAHOMA
Route 66, Oklahoma City

M.A. Doran, Tulsa

OREGON
Bibelot, Portland

PENNSYLVANIA
Glass Growers, Erie
Stone Heart, Lafayette Hill
Artisans Gallery, Lahaska
Sawtooth, Lancaster
G Squared, Ligonier
Craftworks, New Hope
American Pie, Philadelphia
Journeys of Life, Pittsburgh
Collage, York

RHODE ISLAND
WAVE Gallery, Newport
O.O.P., Providence

SOUTH CAROLINA
Red Door, Anderson
East Bay Gallery, Charleston
Portfolio Art Gallery, Columbia
Smith Galleries, Hilton Head Island
East Bay Gallery, Mt. Pleasant
Studio 77, Myrtle Beach
Red Piano, Too, St. Helena's Island

TENNESSEE
Monkey Business, Chattanooga
Smith's Crossroads, Dayton
Grandma's Cedar Chest, Dickson
Jonesborough Art Glass, Jonesborogh
Hanson Fine Art & Craft, Knoxville
Artifacts, Memphis
The American Artisan, Nashville

TEXAS
Positive Images, Austin
Art Gallimaufry, Dallas
Iota, Dallas
Artenergies, Fort Worth
Circa Now, Houston
Hanson Galleries, Houston
The Third Floor, Kemah
Southwest Craft Center, San Antonio

UTAH
Coda, Park City

VERMONT
North Wind Artisan's Gallery,
Woodstock

VIRGINIA
LaneSanson, Richmond
Signet Gallery, Charlottesville
Artifax, Norfolk
Artifax Beach, Virginia Beach
Divine Gallery, Hampton

WASHINGTON
FireWorks, Bellingham
Raven Blues, Poulsbo
FireWorks, Seattle

WISCONSIN
Blue Dolphin, Ephraim
Arteffects Gallery, Green Lake
Signe & Co., Hayward
Seebeck Gallery, Kenosha
Perine, Madison
Atypic, Milwaukee
Katie Gingrass Gallery, Milwaukee

CANADA

ALBERTA
Eclectibles, Calgary

BRITISH COLUMBIA
Dragonfly & Amber, Peachland

MANITOBA
Moule, Winnipeg

Notes from People All Over

From people dropping in on-line to chat on the web site at www.storypeople.com, to others dropping in to chat here at the studios in Iowa, we feel as if we've become part of a much greater community. (Ellen & I have always wanted to get all of you StoryPeople together somewhere for one great, rollicking party, because we're so sure you'd enjoy each other immensely...)

All the letters & calls & faxes & e-mails we continue to get tell of how that community is growing, a person at a time, & how much the stories are affecting the way we live in the world. I wanted to show you some excerpts here, but I couldn't choose the best ones. Thousands of letters & they're all wonderful. (Ellen says to tell you that she likes reading the letters more than she likes watching Little House on the Prairie. I guess that says it all...)

So, we're going to put them up on the web site. That way you can read them for yourself. (We don't put anyone's name, by the way, unless they say it's all right. But we do want to share the letters themselves.)

Please feel free to write us. Our contact information is in the front & back of the book. (Some people start at the front, some people start at the back. We wanted to make it easier for everybody. Though I did draw the line at putting it in the middle for those of you who start there.) Ellen & I look forward to hearing from you.

Until then, much love,

About StoryPeople

StoryPeople are wood sculptures, three to four feet tall, in a roughly human form. They can be as varied as a simple cutout figure, or an assemblage of found and scrap wood, or an intricate, roughly made treasure box. Each piece uses only recycled barn and fence wood from old homesteads in the northeast Iowa area. Adding to their individual quirkiness are scraps of old barn tin and twists of wire. They are painted with bright colors and hand-stamped, a letter at a time, with original stories. The most striking aspect of StoryPeople are the shaded spirit faces. These faces are softly blended into the wood surface, and make each StoryPerson come alive.

Every figure is signed and numbered, and is unique because of the materials used. The figures, the colorful story prints, and the books, are available in galleries and stores throughout the US, Canada & the UK. Please feel free to call or write for more information, or drop in at our web site.

StoryPeople
P.O. Box 7
Decorah, IA 52101 USA

800.476.7178
319.382.8060
319.382.0263 FAX

orders@storypeople.com
http://www.storypeople.com